Collins

My First Book of

Myths
and
Legends

**Collins My First Book of
Myths and Legends**

Collins
An imprint of HarperCollins Publishers
Westerhill Road
Bishopbriggs
Glasgow G64 2QT

© HarperCollins Publishers 2013
Maps © Collins Bartholomew Ltd 2013

ISBN 978-0-00-752123-4
ISBN 978-0-00-752304-7

Imp 001

The contents of this edition of Collins My First Book
of Myths and Legends are believed correct at the time
of printing. Nevertheless the publishers can accept
no responsibility for errors or omissions, changes
in the detail given, or for any expense or loss
thereby caused.

British Library Cataloguing in Publication Data
A catalogue record for this book is available from the
British Library.

Printed and bound by Printing Express,
Hong Kong

All mapping in this atlas is generated from Collins
Bartholomew digital databases.
Collins Bartholomew, the UK's leading independent
geographical information supplier, can provide a
digital, custom, and premium mapping service to a
variety of markets.
For further information:
Tel: +44 (0) 141 306 3752
e-mail: collinsbartholomew@harpercollins.co.uk

Visit our websites at:
www.harpercollins.co.uk
www.collinsbartholomew.com
www.collinsmaps.com

Contents

Introduction

My First Book of Myths and Legends is a selection of stories from around the world. Some are well known favourites and others may be less familiar, but all are fascinating reading for any young reader.

Every culture has a favourite story to tell. Most people have favourite childhood stories which are often fascinating and frightening. Some have a few true facts but many have been passed on from person to person many times and the truth is changed over the years.

Stories, many of which are known as myths or legends, are told all over the world and the place they are from may be very important to the story and the people who created them.

A legend is a story that is only semi-true but has an important meaning for the culture from which it originated. It usually features a hero or heroine or it may be based on a real historic event.

Legends usually involve heroic characters or fantastic places and often encompass the spiritual beliefs of the culture in which they originate.

A myth is a story based on a tradition, which has a symbolic meaning. A myth does not necessarily record a true event but does 'convey a truth' to those who tell it and hear it.

Sometimes, it is difficult to know if a story is a myth or a legend. All of them have at some time helped people understand their relationship with the world around them. Some of them still do to this day.

Stories from the World

Stories from Europe

9

Romulus and Remus

Rhea was a princess, the daughter of Numitor, rightful ruler of the kingdom of Alba Longa. But Numitor was killed by his brother, Amulius, who forced Rhea into hiding.

She was visited by Mars, the Roman god of war, and later gave birth to twin sons, Romulus and Remus. Amulius cast the boys adrift in a basket on the River Tiber to die.

But the twins were saved – by a she-wolf. Miraculously, the she-wolf took Romulus and Remus to her cave and suckled them like her cubs.

Later, a shepherd and his wife found the twins. The couple fostered the boys to manhood, but as they got older they wanted to be kings not simple shepherds.

When the twins discovered the truth of their birth they killed Amulius and restored their grandfather Numitor to his throne. Rather than wait to inherit Alba Longa they decided to found a new city on the shores of the Tiber.

Romulus wanted the new city to be on the Palatine Hill; Remus preferred the Aventine Hill. They both wanted to be the only king. They quarrelled and in a fit of rage Romulus picked up a rock and killed his brother.

Romulus founded the new city, which he named Roma, after himself. He created its first legions and senate, and became the great city's first king.

Pandora's Box

Epimetheus and his brother, Prometheus, lived on Earth a long time ago. They were kind men and Prometheus helped people learn how to create fire. This got them in trouble with Zeus, king of the gods, who didn't want people to know how to do this.

To punish the brothers for this Zeus had a beautiful woman created by a man called Hephaestus. This woman was called Pandora, and she was sent down to earth to meet the brothers. She was very charming as well as beautiful and Epimetheus fell in love with her and married her.

As a wedding gift Zeus sent Epimetheus a box. This box came with a message from the gods that it was never to be opened.

The gods were hoping that Epimetheus would be too curious to leave the box unopened. However, it was Pandora who was most curious and one day she could wait no longer and opened the box.

Pandora imagined that there would be great riches in the box but when she opened it all that was in there were some moths. As this box was from the gods the moths represented all the awful things in the world and Pandora had let them all loose. She closed the box as quickly as she could but it was too late.

When her husband returned she told him what she had done and opened the box to show him. There was one small moth left in the box which was 'hope' and they released this into the world too.

Thor and Loki

Thor was the Norse god of thunder and the sky. Thursday is named after him. Thor wielded the mountain-crushing hammer, Mjollnir, which returned to him like a boomerang when he threw it. He was known for his hot temper and huge appetite.

Loki was a trickster god and shape shifter, prone to mischief.

Thor's main enemies were the frost giants. When people heard thunder and saw lightning, they knew Thor was fighting these evil foes.

On one occasion Thrym, the giant king, seized Mjollnir and said he would only return it if the beautiful goddess Freyja married him. Freyja refused, so Loki hatched a plan. He dressed Thor in women's clothing and a bridal veil to disguise him as Freyja. Loki then led 'Freyja' to Jotunheim, the home of the giants.

Thrym welcomed his 'bride', but was mightily surprised by her appetite at the wedding feast. She ate a whole ox and drank three barrels of wine just for starters! Loki said she hadn't eaten for a week because she had been too excited about marrying Thrym.

The giant fell for this fib and continued with the ceremony. But when it was time to place a hammer in the bride's lap, as custom dictated, Thor threw off his bridal outfit. He grabbed Mjollnir back and used it to smash the giants and wreck their hall.

St George and the Dragon

Saint George was a knight whose travels took him to Silene in Libya. This place had a terrible secret – in a large lake by the town lived a dragon.

No crueller beast had ever been seen. The deadly monster had rough green scales as hard as iron and huge wings that blotted out the sun. Its rank breath had poisoned the land all about.

At first the townspeople gave the dragon two sheep a day to stop it attacking them. But they ran out of sheep and in their desperation they began to offer their children to it. The unfortunate human sacrifices were chosen by lottery.

When the king's daughter, Princess Sadra, was selected, the king offered gold to spare her. But the townspeople demanded that she be delivered to the dragon just as many of their children had been.

So the king dressed Sadra in a wedding gown, and led her out to be fed to the dragon.

George was then passing by and he asked Sadra what was happening. She begged him to leave before the dragon appeared and killed him too.

But George swore that he would help Sadra, in the name of Jesus. Just then the mighty dragon reared out of the lake. George charged it on his horse and stabbed it deeply with his spear.

He took the lady's girdle and tied it round the dragon's neck. The beast followed Sadra meekly into the city like a dog on a lead.

The people were terrified, but George calmed them, and called on them to be baptised as Christians. They were, and George then slew the dragon. Its huge body was carried out of the city on four ox-carts.

The king built a church to the Blessed Virgin Mary and Saint George, and from its altar rose a spring that cured all disease.

Theseus and the Minotaur

Minos, the powerful ruler of Crete, had captured Athens and demanded a terrible tribute. Every nine years the people of Athens must send him seven maidens and seven youths.

These victims were cast into the Labyrinth, a twisting maze that was impossible to escape from. There they would be devoured by the Minotaur – a half bull, half human monster.

Theseus, son of Aegeus, King of Athens, offered to be one of the victims so he could slay the monster. He set off in a boat with a black sail, telling his father that if he were successful he would return under a white sail.

The victims arrived in Crete and Ariadne, King Minos' daughter, fell in love with Theseus as he was paraded past her. She begged Daedalus, the designer of the maze, for help and he gave her a ball of thread.

Ariadne gave the thread to Theseus in return for a promise of marriage. When Theseus entered the Labyrinth, he tied the thread to the doorpost, unravelling it as he walked.

Theseus came to the heart of the Labyrinth where the Minotaur lay sleeping. The beast woke and the two fought ferociously. Theseus strangled the Minotaur and followed the thread safely out of the Labyrinth. He led the victims and Ariadne to his ship and set sail for Athens.

Unfortunately, Ariadne died on the return journey. Theseus was so upset he forgot to put up the white sail. King Aegeus saw the black sail approaching and threw himself off a cliff and into the sea. That sea has been called the Aegean ever since.

Odysseus and his Extraordinary Journey

Odysseus was one of the greatest Greek leaders in the ten-year Trojan War. It was his idea to build a huge wooden horse and fill it with soldiers, which helped the Greeks capture Troy. Victorious, Odysseus and his twelve ships of men set off for home. It would be another ten years of peril and adventure before he arrived to take his place as rightful King of Ithaca.

The Cyclops

The travellers were captured by a man-eating Cyclops, which devoured several sailors. Odysseus gave the Cyclops a barrel of wine and the monster drank it and fell asleep. Then Odysseus set fire to a wooden stake using the remaining wine, and burned the Cyclops' one eye, blinding him.

Circe

Only Odysseus' ship remained of the fleet when they visited the seductive witch-goddess Circe. She turned half of the remaining men into pigs. Odysseus used a magic drug to resist Circe's magic. Amazed at his powers, she fell in love with him and released his men. They feasted on the island for a whole year before finally leaving for Ithaca.

Scylla and Charybdis

Scylla was a six-headed monster and Charybdis a fearsome whirlpool, very close to Scylla. Odysseus directed his men to row directly between the two. But Scylla seized the ship's oars and ate six men.

Calypso

When Odysseus' men ignored warnings not to hunt the sun god's sacred cattle, their folly led to Odysseus' ship being destroyed by a thunderbolt. Only Odysseus survived, washing ashore on the island of the nymph Calypso. She forced him to remain as her lover for seven years before he finally escaped.

Ithaca

Eventually Odysseus made it home, after twenty years away. But he still had to contend with several greedy suitors who were pestering his faithful wife, Penelope. With the help of his son and father, Odysseus slaughtered the suitors and eventually restored peace.

Hercules and Cerberus

Hercules was a mighty warrior who was set twelve terrifying tasks by King Eurystheus. The final one of these was the most deadly of all: find the vicious beast Cerberus that guarded the Underworld, also known as Hades, and kidnap it.

Cerberus had three heads, a dragon for a tail, and snake heads all over his back. Hades was where people's spirits went to when they died. It lay in the bowels of the earth and no living soul had ever returned from its depths.

Through a deep, rocky cave, Hercules made his way into Hades. He encountered monsters, heroes and ghosts. Finally he found Pluto, Lord of the Underworld, and asked him for Cerberus. Pluto agreed, provided that Hercules overpowered the beast without weapons.

Undaunted, the hero threw his strong arms around the beast. The dragon in the tail plunged its teeth into Hercules, but that did not stop the valiant warrior. Hercules wrestled Cerberus into submission and carried the monster back up to our world.

King Eurystheus was so

Stories from America

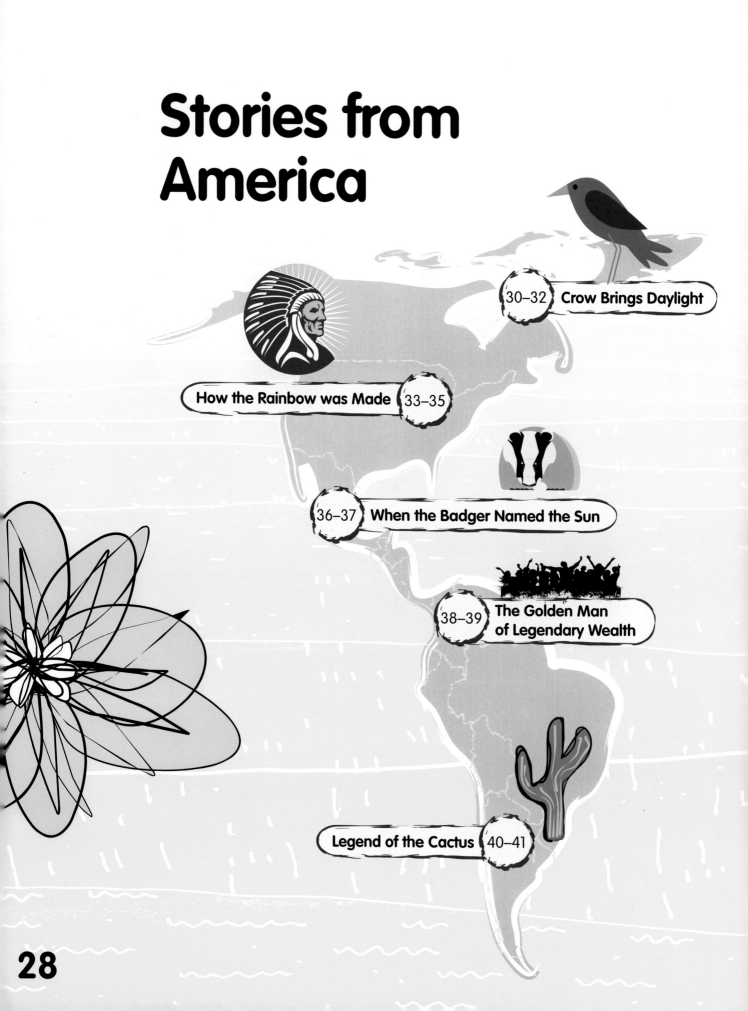

Crow Brings Daylight

When the world was first born, it was always dark in the land of the Inuit. They thought it was the same everywhere until an old crow told them he had seen daylight in the south.

'If we had daylight we could hunt for longer,' the people said. They begged Crow to bring them the daylight.

Crow flew south until at last he came to the light. He rested in a tree by a river as a beautiful girl came to dip her bucket in the water. Crow turned himself into a speck of dust and drifted into the girl's fur cloak.

She returned to the snow lodge of her father, the chief. Inside, the speck of dust drifted towards the chief's favourite grandson, who was playing on the lodge floor. It floated into the child's ear and he started to cry.

'Why are you crying?' asked the chief, who was sitting at the fire.

'Tell him you want to play with a ball of daylight,' whispered the dust.

The chief told his daughter to fetch the box of daylight balls. He took out a small ball, wrapped a string around it and gave it to his favourite grandson.

The speck of dust scratched the child's ear again, making him cry.

'What's wrong, child?' asked the chief.

'Tell him you want to play outside,' whispered the dust.

As they all left the snow lodge, the speck of dust turned back into Crow who flew off with the ball of daylight. At the land of the Inuit, Crow dropped the ball, and it shattered. The sky grew bright, dark mountains took on colour, the snow sparkled and the people were delighted. 'We can see for miles! Thank you, Crow!'

Crow said: 'I could only carry one small ball of daylight. You'll only have daylight for half the year.'

The people said: 'Half a year is plenty – before you brought daylight, we lived our whole life in darkness!'

To this day, the Inuit live half a year in darkness and half a year in daylight. And they are always kind to Crow.

How the Rainbow was Made

One day when the earth was new, Nanabozho looked out of his house beside the waterfall and realized that all the flowers in his meadow were pale. How boring! He gathered up his paints and his paintbrushes and went out.

Nanabozho sat down in the meadow grass and painted the flowers. He painted the violets dark blue, the lilies orange, the roses red, the daffodils yellow and the pansies every colour he could think of.

Nanabozho looked up to see two little birds playing. As the first bird soared past Nanabozho, his right wing dipped into the red paint pot. The second playful bird's wing grazed the orange paint pot.

Nanabozho scolded the two birds, but they kept up their game. Soon their feet and feathers were covered with paint of all colours. Finally Nanabozho stood up and shooed the birds away.

The birds zoomed over the giant waterfall next to Nanabozho's house. Zippity-zip, they flew through the misty spray of the waterfall and began to streak the sky in different colours!

Brother Sun shone and the brilliant colours formed a gorgeous arch of red and orange and yellow and green and blue and violet in the sky above the waterfall. Nanabozho smiled at the little birds and said: 'You have made a rainbow!'

From that day to this, whenever Brother Sun shines his light on the rain or the mist, a beautiful rainbow forms. It is a reflection of the mighty rainbow that still stands over the waterfall at Nanabozho's house.

When the Badger Named the Sun

A long time ago, nobody knew the name of the sun. The people wanted to know what to call this familiar face that rose in the sky every day and gave them warmth. So they held a meeting on the banks of the Surem river.

Their biggest problem was that they couldn't decide if the sun was a man or a woman. Everyone had their own idea, but nobody could say for sure.

'Let's ask the animals,' said the people eventually. So they called all the animals of the world to join the meeting.

Birds and beasts gathered by the tumbling blue waters of the river before daybreak. There had never been such a huge group of men and animals!

When the sun appeared, everyone fell silent in wonder. Then a badger came out of the hole in the ground where he lived.

He shuffled over to the meeting and said in a loud voice, 'The sun rises from the earth like I come out of my hole, so he must be male.'

'Oh, badger!' they cried. 'You've done it!' Everyone was so impressed that they started cheering and clapping. They decided to throw a huge party in the badger's honour.

But the badger took fright at the noise. He ran back into his hole and refused to come out. He thought they wanted to punish him.

To this day, a badger spends most of his time in his hole, scared that everyone is angry with him.

The Golden Man of Legendary Wealth

In the land that is now Colombia, the Muisca tribe once had a spectacular way of crowning a new king.

At the mystical Lake Guatavita, the people made a raft of rushes, which they decorated beautifully. The new king was stripped of clothes and anointed with sticky, fragrant oil. He stepped onto the raft. A great heap of gold and some emeralds was piled at his feet, and he was covered from top to toe with gold dust.

He became the Golden Man – 'El Dorado'.

Clouds of fragrant incense sweetened the air. Fires lit up the night and the new king floated over the dark waters. In the centre of the lake he cast the treasures into the depths as offerings to the spirit that the people worshipped.

Pipes and flutes played, and the people danced and sang as he returned to the shore as their new king.

When European invaders came, they heard the Golden Man legend. They assumed that any people who could throw gold away must be incredibly wealthy. The story of El Dorado became transformed into a tale of a kingdom, an empire, and a 'Lost City of Gold' that had belonged to this golden king.

The invaders foolishly squandered much money and many lives looking for what was nothing but a beautiful ceremony.

Legend of the Cactus

Near the mountains there lived a tribe. The most handsome of the young men was Quehualliu. He loved picking flowers for Pasancana, the beautiful daughter of the chief. They spent their childhood days together, roaming freely over the lovely hills and valleys.

When they were older, they realized they had fallen in love. But the chief wanted Pasancana to marry another boy in the tribe who was an excellent hunter. He did not allow Quehualliu and Pasancana to be together.

The lovers cried as they couldn't bear to be apart. The next night they waited until the first star came out and then fled together into the highest mountains.

The chief was furious. He summoned the best hunters and together they searched the hills for the couple.

Meanwhile, Pasancana and Quehualliu were tired, so they sat down for a few minutes. They were drifting off to sleep when the hunting party arrived.

They saw the men by the light of the full moon and begged Pachamama, the goddess of the land, to hide them.

Pachamama took pity on the young lovers. She opened a hole in the mountain and hid them there.

'Don't worry,' the chief shouted. 'They can't hide forever!' He and his men camped outside the hole all night, expecting to find their quarry in the morning.

Dawn brought a surprise for the men. Above the hole a beautiful cactus had appeared. The lovers had been magically transformed, and you can see them in the mountains to this day as a cactus, shaped like Quehualliu protecting Pasancana.

Stories from Africa

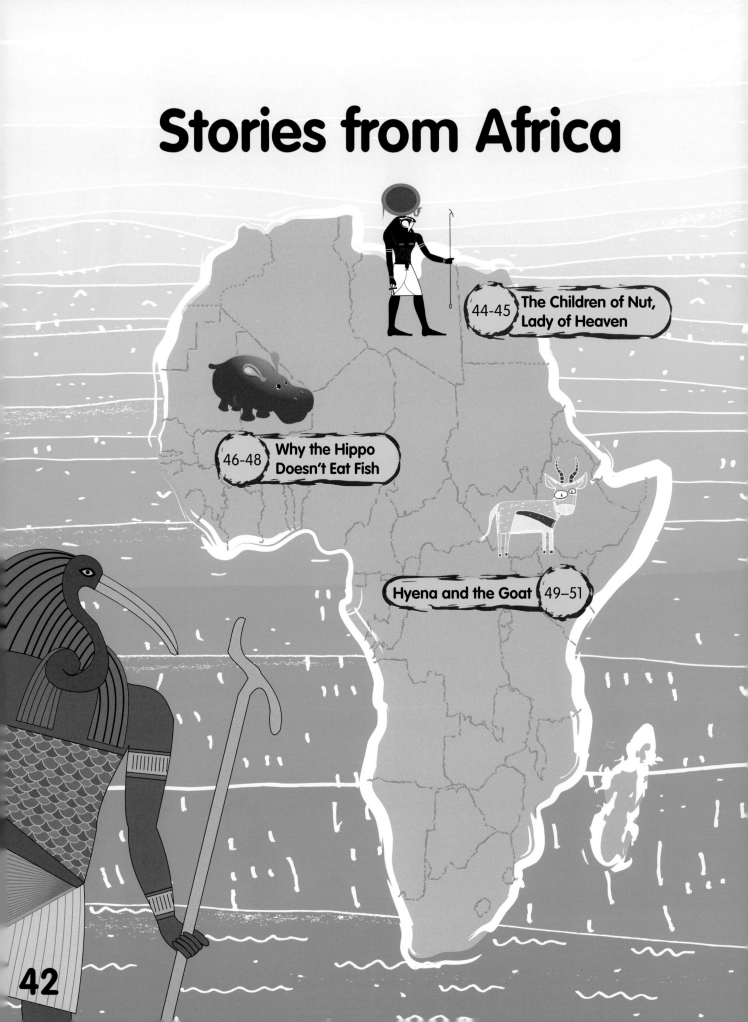

The Children of Nut, Lady of Heaven

Ra was the sun god who made himself mortal to rule the world of men as the first Pharaoh. For years he ruled well and the harvests were bountiful and men honoured him.

Ra grew old and men no longer respected him. He feared someone taking his throne. He longed to know what the future held.

Ra spoke the word 'Thoth' and this brought the god of wisdom into being. Thoth could speak prophecy and Ra asked him what the future held. Thoth said: 'Another ruler of Egypt will replace you. He will be the son of Nut, goddess of the sky.'

Ra was furious. He cursed Nut, saying, 'Nut will not give birth on any day of the year, neither on any night.' At that time, the year was only 360 days.

Nut was heartbroken and she went to Thoth for advice. Thoth agreed to help her if she would marry him. Nut, who secretly loved Thoth, agreed.

Thoth knew that he could not change Ra's curse, but he thought of a way round it. He went to Khonsu the moon-god, gave him beer and honey, and played draughts with him long into the night. Thoth played cleverly and the bets ran ever higher. Eventually Khonsu was forced to bet a piece of his own light.

Thoth eventually won enough of Khonsu's light to make five extra days. Now the year had 365 days.

Khonsu lost so much light that he could not shine fully every night. Every month he was forced to wane to a sliver of light and slowly wax back to his full glory.

Nut and Thoth had five children on the five new days, so avoiding Ra's curse. Osiris was born on the first day and a loud voice was heard all over the world, saying, 'The lord of all the earth is born.' Then Horus, Set, Isis and Nephthys arrived on the following days.

In time, Osiris grew and became a mighty king, replacing Ra as Thoth had predicted.

Why the Hippo Doesn't Eat Fish

Long, long ago, when the world was still young, the Good Lord N'gai made a place for all the creatures upon his earth.

The hippopotamus was free to roam in the forests and plains. There was plenty of food and the greedy hippopotamus soon grew fat. The bigger his belly got, the more he suffered in the African sun.

One fiercely hot day he waddled down to the river. As he gazed at the little fish swimming happily through the cool pools he had a thought. 'Oh,' he sighed, 'I wish I could live in the refreshing water like the fish!'

He shouted up to the heavens.

'Please, Good Lord N'gai,'
he bellowed, 'your fiery sun
is burning me up! Let me
leave the roasting plains
and live in your cool rivers.'

Lord N'gai looked at hippopotamus's
big mouth, long teeth and hungry belly.

'No,' replied Lord N'gai, 'I love my fish and if you
lived in the rivers and lakes, you would eat them.
It has to be dry land for you, hippopotamus.'

At this news, the hippopotamus began weeping
and wailing. He made the most awful noise,
begging Lord N'gai to change his mind.

The Great Lord N'gai looked down upon the plains baking in the heat of the tropical sun. Eventually his heart softened.

'Very well, hippopotamus,' he said, 'I will let you live in my rivers and lakes, but you must swear never to eat my little fish.'

'Oh great Lord N'gai,' cried hippopotamus, 'I promise most faithfully that I will eat only grass, never a single fish. And every day I will prove this to you, my lord.'

'So be it,' said Lord N'gai and hippopotamus galloped down the riverbank and splashed into the stream, grunting with delight.

So to this day, hippos always scatter their dung on the riverbank, so Lord N'gai can see that it contains no fish bones. And you can still hear them roaring with joy that they are allowed to live in the cool waters.

Hyena and the Goat

When Goat was returning from the market with a bag of salt she met hungry Hyena. To hide her fear she decided to pretend Hyena was her uncle.

'Hello Uncle,' said Goat.

Hyena did not know that he was related to any goats. He stopped to think about all the members of his family.

While he was thinking, Goat turned quickly and hid in a nearby cave where she knew Lion was recovering from a broken leg.

Hyena followed Goat, but didn't know that Lion was inside. The three of them met face to face. Goat thought quickly, and taking the salt she had bought in the market, she faced Lion and proudly announced:

'Lion, I have brought you a cure for your broken leg. You must eat salted Hyena meat. See here, I have brought you the salt'.

Lion looked at the salt and said:

'It is good of you to have brought the salt, and I see that there is also a Hyena here'.

With one giant paw Lion reached out and knocked Hyena to the floor. He took a bite out of his back, rubbed the flesh in the salt and swallowed it. He loved the taste, so asked Goat if he could have some more.

'Certainly' Goat replied, 'you can keep it all!' and slowly backed out of the cave before running off to safety.

Lion took a second bite out of Hyena's back. While he rubbed the second piece of meat in the salt, Hyena took his chance and escaped from the cave. Until this day, Hyena still walks with a low back because of the mouthfuls that Lion took out of him.

Stories from Oceania

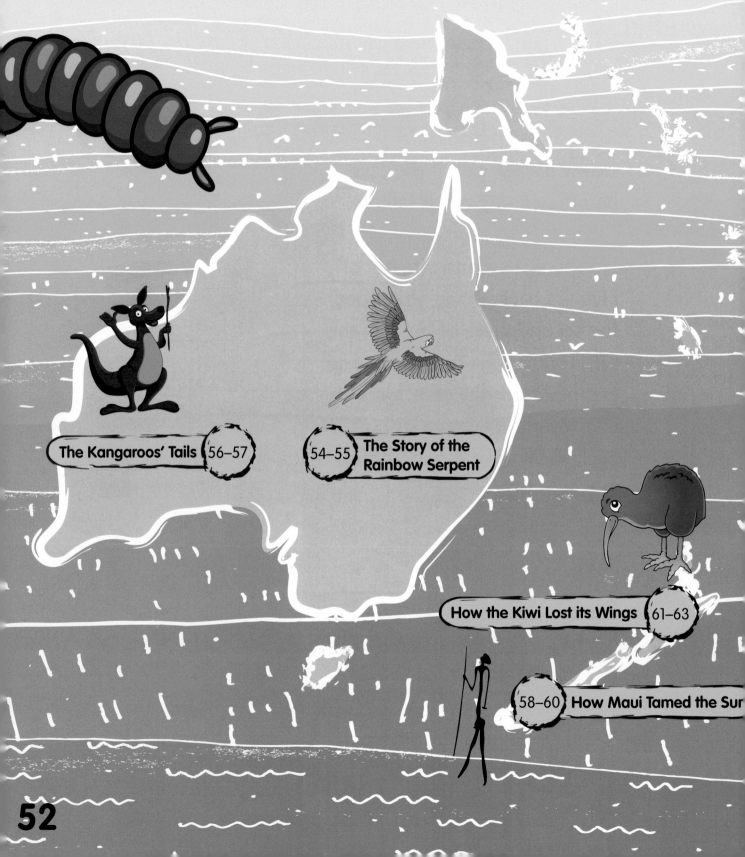

53

The Story of the Rainbow Serpent

Way back in Dreamtime, there were only people –
no animals or birds, no trees or bushes, no hills or
mountains. Goorialla, the Great Rainbow Serpent,
felt lonely in the wilderness so he set off across
Australia in search of his people.

In the southeast it was cold in winter.
Snow fell and melted on Goorialla's
bright scales. It dripped to the ground
and became the great rivers.

He travelled northwest where it was
hot and dry. There Goorialla shed
his skin. It made great cliffs. Then he
turned and slithered inland, making waves in
the sand. These made the great sandy deserts.
Goorialla rested in holes he dug. The rains filled
up these holes, meaning that there is always water
in the desert even if it lies deep below the ground.

One day at the meeting place of two rivers,
Goorialla came upon a tribe singing and dancing.

'Come and join us!' they cried. Goorialla showed the people new dances and fine ways to dress.

That night a big storm came, and two boys asked to share Goorialla's shelter. But there was no room. So Goorialla opened his mouth and sheltered the boys in his big body.

Then he became worried – what would the tribe say when they found the boys missing? They would be angry. So Goorialla ran away.

In the morning the tribe followed his twisting tracks in the wet ground. They found Goorialla on a mountain top and cut open his stomach. The boys came out, but they had turned into rainbow-coloured birds, called lorikeets.

Goorialla fled, shedding his whole skin on the mountain top. He dived into the east sea and his body became the great reef. You can see it to this day.

And after rain you can see his rainbow skin, curving over the mountain. That is why he is called Goorialla the Rainbow Serpent.

The Kangaroos' Tails

In the early days of Dreamtime there were two kangaroos. Little kangaroo came from the hills and was small with short arms and short legs. Big kangaroo was from the plains and had long arms and long legs.

One day little kangaroo reached into a hole in the rock and when he pulled out his paw it was covered in sugarbag. He licked the golden bush honey. It was delicious. Big kangaroo saw this and he fancied some sugarbag for himself. Little kangaroo said, 'Reach in and get some.'

Big kangaroo thrust his long arms deep into the hole and pulled out a handful of spiders.

'Try again,' said little kangaroo.

Big kangaroo thrust his paws into the hole, but again he pulled out only spiders. Little kangaroo kept reaching his short paws just inside the hole and pretty soon he'd eaten all the sugarbag.

Big kangaroo was furious. He grabbed up a stick and hit little kangaroo on the head with it. Little kangaroo grabbed a bigger stick and hit him back.

Big kangaroo ran off but little kangaroo threw his stick and its point stuck into the back of big kangaroo. Big kangaroo was really angry and threw his stick too. It stuck point-first into little kangaroo.

They both decided enough was enough and took off back into their own country.

Now when you see kangaroos from the hills and plains, you'll know how they got their tails.

How Maui Tamed the Sun

When the Sun was younger he rose more quickly and sped faster across the sky than he does now.

A boy called Maui heard his older brothers complain about how this meant there wasn't enough sunlight during the day. There was never enough light to hunt, fish and do jobs, no matter how early they got up.

Maui thought deeply about this. Then one night as his brothers sat round the fire complaining as usual, he said: 'I can tame the Sun.'

They laughed.

'Maui, don't be daft!' they replied. 'You would be burnt to a cinder. He's too big and powerful. No one can tame the Sun.' 'Listen,' said Maui, 'go with the women and collect as much flax as you possibly can. Then I will show you.'

His brothers were so
curious they collected
a huge mound of flax.
Maui showed them
how to plait it into long,
strong ropes. He then
tied these together into a gigantic net.
He picked up his axe and said: 'Follow me.'

For days they walked eastwards. They found the cave
from which the Sun would rise next morning and
they covered the entrance with their net. Then Maui
made them plaster themselves in wet clay and hide.

Soon they saw the first glimmer of light from the
cave. Then they felt the scorching heat. The brothers
shook with fear as the blinding furnace
rose up. But the clay kept them cool.

59

Then Maui shouted, 'Pull!'

The mighty net trapped the Sun.

The Sun was furious, and he struggled and roared. Maui ran towards the Sun with his axe held high.

The Sun roared even louder: 'Why are you trying to kill me?'

'I'm not,' said Maui, 'but you must understand. You go too fast across the sky. We need more hours of light to work.'

'Well,' sighed the Sun, 'you have made me so weak that I can only go slowly now, I promise.'

Maui released the ropes and the Sun rose slowly into the sky. His brothers and the other tribesmen smiled at young Maui – they were proud of him.

To this day, the Sun crosses the sky at a slow pace, giving us time to do all our work.

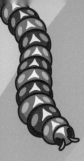

How the Kiwi Lost its Wings

One day, Tanemahuta, the forest god, saw that his children, the trees, were getting sick, as bugs were eating them.

He asked his brother Tanehokahoka, the sky god, to call all the birds together.

Tanemahuta spoke to the gathering of birds.

'Insects are devouring my children, the trees. I need one of you to come down and live on the forest floor to save my children and your home. Who will come down?'

And not one bird spoke.

Tanehokahoka turned to Tui.

'Tui, will you come down from the forest roof?'

Tui looked down at the deep shade beneath the trees and shuddered. 'It is too dark.'

Tanehokahoka turned to Pukeko.

'Pukeko, will you come down from the forest roof?'

Pukeko looked down at the wet earth on the forest floor and shuddered. 'It is too damp.'

Tanehokahoka turned to Pipiwharauroa.

'Pipiwharauroa, will you come down from the forest roof?'

Pipiwharauroa looked around and saw his family.

'I am too busy building my nest.'

All was quiet, and not a bird spoke, and great was the sadness in the heart of Tanehokahoka. At last he turned to Kiwi.

'Kiwi, will you come down from the forest roof?'

Kiwi looked up at the sunlit trees, looked around and saw his family. Kiwi then looked at the cold, damp earth. He turned to Tanehokahoka and said, 'I will.'

Tanehokahoka and Tanemahuta were filled with joy, for this little bird was giving them hope. But Tanemahuta felt that he should warn Kiwi of what would happen.

'Kiwi, do you know that you will grow thick legs to live on the ground? That you will lose your coloured feathers? That you will never again fly and see the light of day?'

'I know,' said Kiwi.

Then Tanehokahoka turned to the other birds and said:

'Tui, because you were too scared to come down you will always wear two white feathers at your throat as the mark of a coward.'

'Pukeko, because you did not want to get your feet wet, you will live forever in the swamp.'

'Pipiwharauroa, because you were too busy building your nest, you will never build another nest again, but lay your eggs in other birds' nests.'

'But you, Kiwi, because of your great sacrifice, you will become the most well-known and most loved bird of them all.'

63

Stories from Asia

The Mice that Ate the Iron

A young merchant was heading off on a long trip. He had to travel light, so he took his precious iron weighing scales to a nearby shopkeeper and asked the man to look after them.

'Certainly,' said the shopkeeper.

When the merchant returned from his trip he went back to the shopkeeper to collect his scales.

'I'm sorry,' said the shopkeeper. 'I'm afraid the mice have eaten them.'

'Eaten them?' cried the astonished merchant. 'They were solid iron!'

'It does seem odd,' said the shopkeeper. 'But the mice around here love the taste of iron. Especially fine quality iron like that.'

The merchant thought hard as he walked home. 'That can't be true. No mouse ever ate iron. That crafty shopkeeper just wants my scales for himself. But how can I prove it?'

The next morning, the merchant went for a cooling swim in the lake. He was still puzzling over the scales when he saw the shopkeeper's son swimming in front of him. He had an idea.

The merchant got out and ran as fast as he could to the shopkeeper's house. He hammered on the door.

'Disaster!' he yelled. 'I was swimming at the lake and a huge crow swooped down and carried off your son!'

'What?' gasped the shopkeeper, running out and looking frantically at the sky. Then he frowned. 'That can't be true,' he said. 'No crow ever carried a person off.'

The merchant shrugged and said: 'In a land where mice are strong enough to eat iron, I'm sure a crow could easily fly away with your son.'

The shopkeeper burned red with shame. He went inside and brought out the scales.

The merchant smiled and took them home and never again did the shopkeeper tell him a lie.

The Story of the Phoenix

One day in the early times, the Sun looked down and saw a large bird with shiny red and gold feathers. The Sun called out, 'Glorious Phoenix, you shall be my bird and live forever!'

The happy Phoenix lifted its head and sang, 'Glorious Sun, I shall sing my songs for you alone!'

When people saw the Phoenix they chased it, desperate to take its beautiful feathers for themselves and to hear its song.

'I cannot live here,' thought the Phoenix. And it flew off to the far eastern desert to praise the Sun in peace.

After five hundred years the Phoenix was old and tired. It wanted to soar high in the sky and fly fast like it did when it was young.

So the Phoenix flew west, and on its journey it collected cinnamon twigs and fragrant leaves, tucking them in its feathers. It picked up a ball of resin in its claws.

Then it flew to Heliopolis
in Egypt, the 'City of the Sun'.
It built a nest on top of the
Temple of the Sun out of the
spices and resin it had
collected on its journey.

The Phoenix sat in its
nest and sang, 'Sun,
glorious Sun, make me
young and strong again!'

In a flash of flame the Sun ignited the nest. The Phoenix was
ablaze and died in the fire.

The flames died down. The ashes trembled and a new, young
Phoenix rose up. It sang to the Sun and as it sang it grew.
When its song ended, it was the same size as the old Phoenix.

Then it spread its wings and flew back to its lonely desert. It
lives there still. But every five hundred years, when it feels old,
it flies west to be burnt by the Sun at the Temple.

And each time, the Phoenix rises from the ashes, young again.

Yin and Yang

Once there was nothing but chaos. It was like a mist full of emptiness. Suddenly, a colourful light burst through the mist and all things that exist in the world came to be.

The mist shook and everything that was light rose up to form heaven and all that which was heavy sank down to become the earth.

Now the forces of heaven and earth came out to produce yin and yang. Yin was like a soft cloud – cool, moist, female, drifting gently. Yang was like a dragon – hot, fiery, male, bursting with energy. Each force had incredible power. On their own they would blast the world back to chaos. But when they are together they are in balance and the world is in harmony.

From this harmony of yin and yang everything is born. The moon is of yin, the sun is of yang.

They worked together to create seasons, elements and living creatures.

On the plain ball of the earth they created the giant P'an Ku, the Ancient One. P'an Ku dug the river valleys and piled up the mountains. For thousands of years he toiled to shape the earth.

When he died at the end of his labours, his body became the five sacred mountains. His hair grew to be the plants and his blood flowed as the rivers. Now his sweat was the rain and it washed away his flakes of skin and they became human beings.

People first lived in caves but soon they learned to build houses. They made tools and boats, learnt to fish, to plough and plant, and they made enough food and lived together in peace.

And all their life is balance. All is thanks to Yin and Yang.

The Adventures of Sinbad

Sinbad was a young man from Baghdad who inherited a fortune from his father. Sadly, he wasted every penny.

So he went to sea to make money. He boarded a trading ship and on its first voyage the crew set ashore on a beautiful island. They lit a fire to camp for the night.

Suddenly the whole island began to shake.

'Run!' yelled the captain. 'This is no island but a huge whale. It has been sleeping so long that trees have grown on it. It is going to dive into the depths of the sea'

The sailors ran for the ship but Sinbad didn't make it. The whale dived deep, the ship sailed off and Sinbad had to cling to a barrel. He drifted for days until he landed safely on an island.

On another adventure he was on a merchant ship that dropped anchor in a bay of a desert island. Far in the distance was a white dome and as they got nearer they could see it was a huge egg.

Sinbad warned the merchants not to touch the egg, but they broke it and took out the chick. As they put the chick in their cooking pot, the sky grew dark.

A huge and horrible bird, the roc, was attacking them to save its child.

They all fled back to the ship but the furious mother roc seized a giant boulder in her talons and dropped it from the clouds, smashing a hole in their vessel. The ship sank like a stone.

Sinbad had seven action-packed voyages in all. Eventually he earned his fortune and returned to Baghdad to live a life of ease and pleasure.

Activity

Can you lead the crow to daylight? Solution on page 79.

75

Activity

Can you find 10 differences? Answers on page 79.

Index

Answers

1. Missing buttons on Hercules' belt
2. Thumb missing on Hercules' hand
3. Ra's rod facing the opposite direction
4. Ra's armband is missing
5. Serpent missing one eye
6. Missing button on Sinbad's headwear
7. Sinbad's shoes now red
8. Crow's beak now yellow
9. Crow has only one leg
10. Paintbrush tip now green

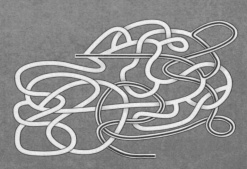

Acknowledgements

Image credits

All images credited unless unknown.

Cover image and title page © Fotokostic/Shutterstock.com

For contents, introduction, mapping and activity page images, see individual stories.
All mapping backgrounds © VOOK/Shutterstock.com

P10 Background © Polina Katritch/Shutterstock.com
P11 Romulus and Remus © Franco Volpato/Shutterstock.com

P12 Background © Hermin/Shutterstock.com
P12 Prometheus © bebenov/Shutterstock.com
P13 Pandora © Osijan/Shutterstock.com
P13 Spiral © vlastas/Shutterstock.com

P14 Thor © Erick S./Shutterstock.com
P14 Monster © Memo Angeles/Shutterstock.com
P15 Loki © mhatzapa/Shutterstock.com

P16-18 Background and Dragon © Litvinova Oxana/Shutterstock.com

P19-21 Background © pashabo/Shutterstock.com
P19 Islands © Merkushev Vasiliy/Shutterstock.com
P20 Theseus © Christos Georghiou/Shutterstock.com
P20 Maze © ensiferum/Shutterstock.com
P21 Diving man © gudron/Shutterstock.com
P21 Ship © AlexeyZet/Shutterstock.com

P22-24 Background © pashabo/Shutterstock.com
P22 Trojan horse © Petr Novotny/Shutterstock.com
P23 Cyclops © IvanNikulin/Shutterstock.com
P23 Circe © Pushkin/Shutterstock.com
P23 Pigs © Igor Zakowski/Shutterstock.com
P24 Scylla © Potapov Alexander/Shutterstock.com
P24 Ship © DankaLilly/Shutterstock.com
P24 Ithaca © Malchev/Shutterstock.com

P25-27 Hades, Cerberus and background © Chimponzee/Shutterstock.com
P27 Hercules © Malchev/Shutterstock.com

P30, 32 Eskimo © vichvarupa/Shutterstock.com
P31 Crow © TeddyandMia/Shutterstock.com
P32 Background © zzveillust/Shutterstock.com

P33 Background © goccedicolore.it/Shutterstock.com
P33 Native American © patrimonio designs ltd/Shutterstock.com
P34-35 Background © goccedicolore.it/Shutterstock.com
P34 Bird © goccedicolore.it/Shutterstock.com

P36 Background © Sapik/Shutterstock.com
P36-37 Animals © Jan Hyrman/Shutterstock.com
P36-37 Birds © animantz/Shutterstock.com

P38-39 Background © Irbena/Shutterstock.com
P38-39 People © Kjpargeter/Shutterstock.com

P40-41 Background © kstudija/Shutterstock.com
P40-41 Flowers and cactus © Filip Miletic/Shutterstock.com
P40-41 People © geographlo/Shutterstock.com
P44-45 Background © pashabo/Shutterstock.com
P40-45 Background © Kudryashka/Shutterstock.com
P44 Ra © pegasusao012/Shutterstock.com
P45 Thoth © TnT Designs/Shutterstock.com

P46-48 Background © Christos Georghiou/Shutterstock.com
P46,48 Hippo © Christos Georghiou/Shutterstock.com
P47 Hand © Michael Monahan/Shutterstock.com

P49-51 Background and animals © VOOK/Shutterstock.com

P54-55 Background © pashabo/Shutterstock.com
P54-55 Rainbow © Tamara Robinson/Shutterstock.com
P54-55 Birds © Yuzach/Shutterstock.com
P54-55 Serpent © annetboreiko/Shutterstock.com

P56-57 Background © benchart/Shutterstock.com
P56-57 Spider © baza178/Shutterstock.com
P56-57 Kangaroos © Sujono sujono/Shutterstock.com

P58-60 Background © Thomas Christoph/Shutterstock.com
P58-60 Men © siloto/Shutterstock.com

P61-63 Background © VeronikaMaskova/Shutterstock.com
P61 Bugs © Buchan/Shutterstock.com
P62-63 Kiwi © Klara Viskova/Shutterstock.com

P66-67 Scales © kavalenkava volha/Shutterstock.com
P66-67 Mice © German Bogomaz/Shutterstock.com
P66 Boy © Matthew Cole/Shutterstock.com
P67 Crow © cartoons/Shutterstock.com

P68-69 Musical notes © PILart/Shutterstock
P68-69 Flames © hugolacasse/Shutterstock
P70 Phoenix © Nina Bortnyk/Shutterstock.com

P70-71 © Trinochka/Shutterstock.com

P72-73 Background and whale © dedMazay/Shutterstock.com
P72 Barrel © John T Takai/Shutterstock.com
P73 Crow foot © cartoons/Shutterstock.com
P73 Rock Klara © Viskova/Shutterstock.com
P73 Boat © Mysterion_Design/Shutterstock.com
P73 Sinbad © notkoo/Shutterstock.com

Text

Main text: Richard Happer